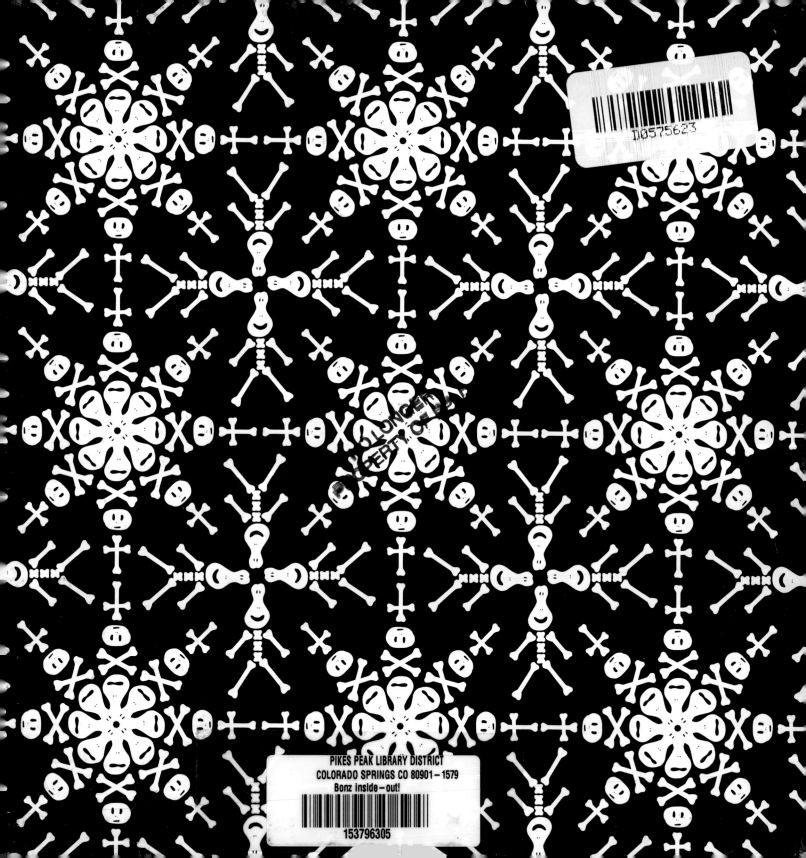

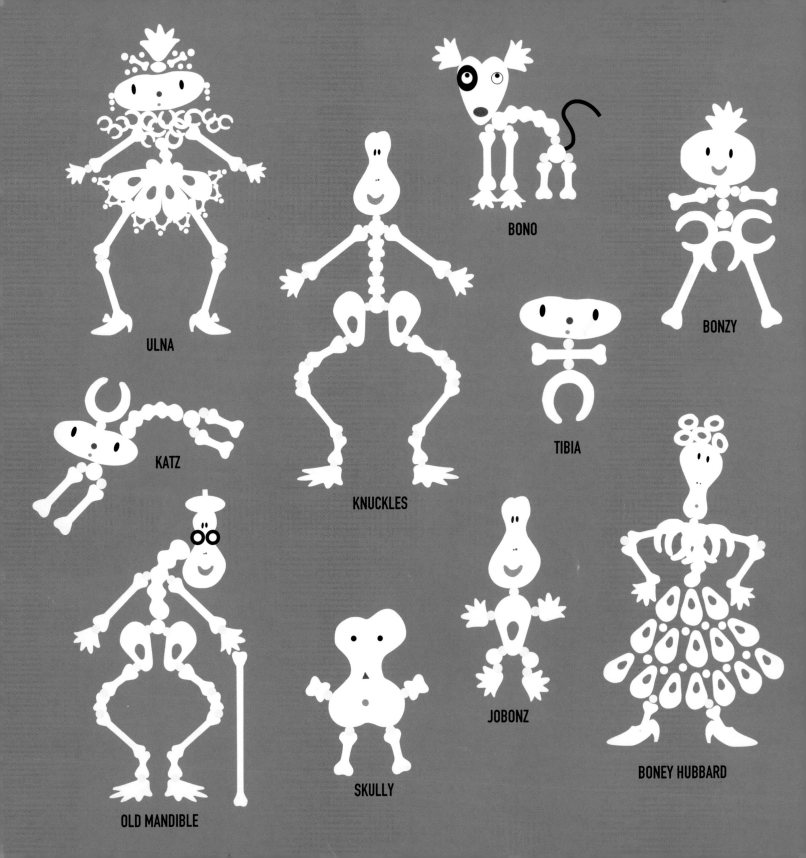

ULNA

BONO

BONZY

KATZ

KNUCKLES

TIBIA

OLD MANDIBLE

SKULLY

JOBONZ

BONEY HUBBARD

BONZ™
iNsiDe-OuT!

a rhythm, rhyme & reason bone-anza!

written & illustrated by

byron glaser & sandra higashi

HARRY N. ABRAMS, INC., PUBLISHERS

Sticks and stones can break my bones...

...but words can tickle my funny Bonz!

Bones help us to dance, fetch, skip
and have fun!

Do you have a
humerus bone in your cranium?
Let's find out!

So heel and toe
and away we go!

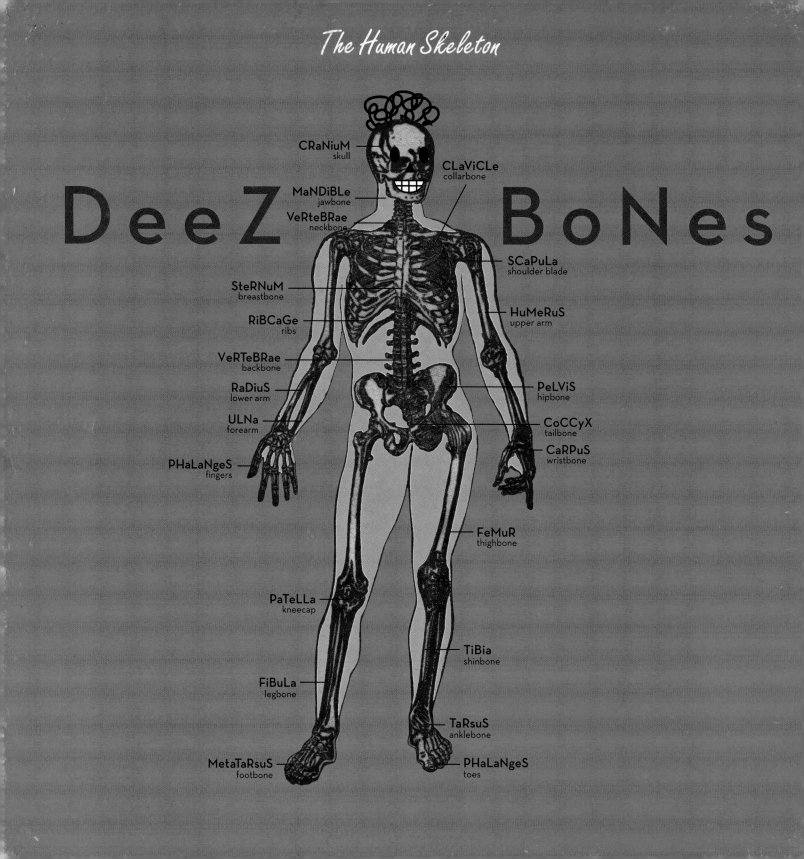

Oh DeM BoNz! DeM BoNz!

DeM  BoNz

ThE hEaD BoNz CoNneCted To tHe NeCk BoNz

tHe NeCk BoNz CoNneCted To tHe SHouLDeR BoNz

thE SHouLDeR BoNz CoNneCted To tHe BaCk BoNz

thE BaCk BoNz CoNneCted To tHe HiP BoNz

tHe HiP BoNz CoNneCted To tHe tHiGh BoNz

thE tHiGh BoNz CoNneCted To tHe kNee BoNz

tHe kNee BoNz CoNneCted To tHe LEg BoNz

THe LeG BoNz CoNneCted To tHe AnKle BoNz

THe AnKle BoNz CoNneCted To tHe FoOT BoNz

Oh DeM BoNz! DeM BoNz!

FUNNY BONZ

Why did the skeleton
run up a tree?

Why was the
skeleton afraid to
cross the road?

Who won the
skeleton beauty contest?

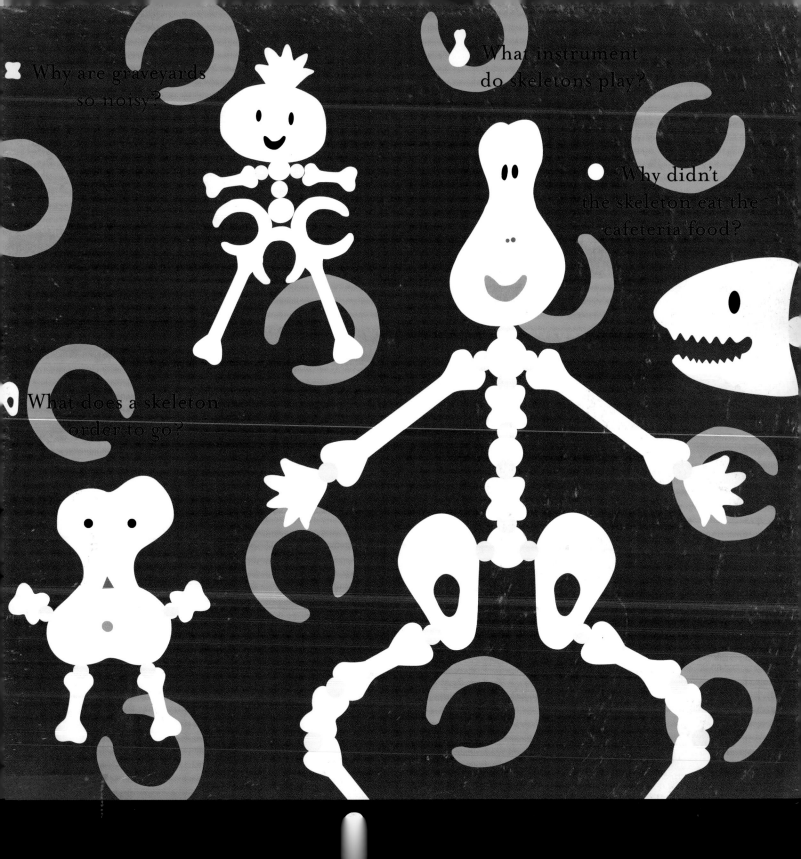

Why are graveyards so noisy?

What instrument do skeletons play?

Why didn't the skeleton eat the cafeteria food?

What does a skeleton order to go?

THE BONEY-HOKEY-POKEY

1 Put your right phalanges in,
put your right phalanges out,

2 Put your right phalanges in
and you shake them all about,

3 You do the boney-hokey-pokey
and you turn yourself around,
that's what it's all about!

4 Put your left phalanges in,
put your left phalanges out,

5 Put your left phalanges in,
and you shake them all about,

6 You do the boney-hokey-pokey
and you turn yourself around,
that's what it's all about!

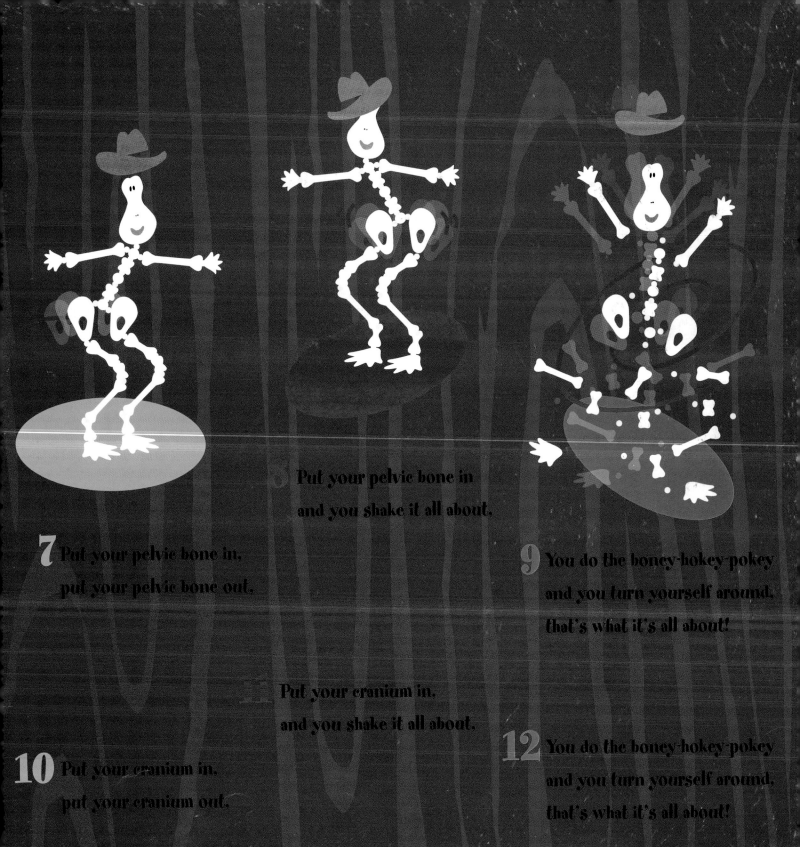

Put your pelvic bone in
and you shake it all about.

7 Put your pelvic bone in,
put your pelvic bone out,

9 You do the boney-hokey-pokey
and you turn yourself around,
that's what it's all about!

Put your cranium in,
and you shake it all about.

10 Put your cranium in,
put your cranium out,

12 You do the boney-hokey-pokey
and you turn yourself around,
that's what it's all about!

THIS OLD MANDIBLE

THIS OLD MANDIBLE, HE PLAYED ONE,

HE PLAYED KNICK–KNACK ON MY THUMB,

WITH A KNICK–KNACK PADDY WHACK GIVE THE DOG A BONE,

THIS OLD MANDIBLE CAME ROLLING HOME.

THIS OLD MANDIBLE, HE PLAYED TWO,

HE PLAYED KNICK–KNACK ON MY SHOE,

WITH A KNICK–KNACK PADDY WHACK GIVE THE DOG A BONE,

THIS OLD MANDIBLE CAME ROLLING HOME.

THIS OLD MANDIBLE, HE PLAYED THREE,

HE PLAYED KNICK–KNACK ON MY KNEE,

WITH A KNICK–KNACK PADDY WHACK GIVE THE DOG A BONE,

THIS OLD MANDIBLE CAME ROLLING HOME.

This Old Mandible, he played four,
He played knick-knack on my door,
With a knick-knack paddy whack give the dog a bone,
This Old Mandible came rolling home.

This Old Mandible, gave high-five!
He played knick-knack to see if I'm alive!
With a knick-knack paddy whack give the dog a bone,
This Old Mandible came rolling home.

S H  O  W

Head and shoulders, knees and toes,
Knees and toes, knees and toes,

Head and shoulders, knees and toes,
Eyes, ears, mouth and nose.

 BONZ!

Ankles, elbows, feet and seat, feet and seat,
Ankles, elbows, feet and seat, feet and seat,

And head and hips and chin and cheeks,
Ankles, elbows, feet and seat, feet and seat.

Old Boney Hubbard went to the cupboard.

To give her poor dog a bone.

But when she got there, her cupboard was bare;

And so the poor dog had none.

She went to the baker's to buy him some bread;

When she got back, the dog was dead.

She went to the undertaker's to buy him a coffin;

When she got back, the dog was a-laughing.

She went to the barber's to buy him a wig;

When she came back, he was dancing a jig.

She went to the tailor's to buy him a coat;

When she came back, he was riding a goat.

She went to the cobbler's to buy him some shoes;

When she came back, he was reading the news.

And in the end he was still really hungry!

Grrrrrrrr.

NEWS FLASH! Today it has been reported that Old Boney Hubbard's cupboard was bare. Sources

Doggone Good Doggie Biscotti

2 cups wheat flour
1/3 cup cornmeal
1/2 cup uncooked oatmeal
1/2 cup ground sunflower seeds
1 tablespoon granulated beef bullion
2 tablespoons olive oil
1/4 cup unsulfured molasses
2 eggs
1/4 cup milk

With an adult's help, combine first 5 ingredients in a bowl. Mix to blend. Add the remaining ingredients. Stir, adding a little more milk if necessary to make a ball that can be kneaded and rolled out on a cutting board. Roll out dough to 1/2 inch thickness. Cut out dog bone shapes with a cardboard stencil or cookie cutter. Place on a well-greased baking sheet. Bake at 350°F for 25 to 35 minutes, or until browned. Cool a few minutes and remove to cooling rack. When cooled completely, give a treat to a hungry doggie friend!

*available in the health section of any major grocery store

THe BiG DiG

find each one of the bonz friends. beware of lookalikes! they must match exactly:

knuckles

ulna

bono

old mandible

bonzy

boney hubbard

tibia

jobonz

skully

katz

BONE-UP!:

fact or fibula?
Different people have different bones.

fact or fibula?
Bones are sometimes rubbery.

fibula! We all have the same basic bones, but we each have a different number of them. The average is about 206, and varies because of the number in our hands and feet.

fact! Bones are soft and rubbery when you are born, and become harder as you age. That's why it hurts an adult more to fall down than a kid!

fact or fibula?

fact or fibula?
Bonz are the same as bones.

fact or fibula?
Skeleton symbols on holidays are always there to scare us.

fact or fibula?
The funny bone is no bone at all.

?

fact! It's actually a tender spot around your elbow, and if you've ever bumped it, you know that it gets tingly and isn't very funny!

fibula! Bonz are imaginary and anatomically incorrect. They don't match the exact size and shape of the bones in your body.

fibula! In Mexico, the festive *Day of the Dead* holiday is celebrated with sugar skulls and skeletons to delight and welcome back the spirits of loved ones.

Día de los Muertos!

How to Celebrate
DAY OF THE DEAD!

IT'S A FIESTA!
A PARTY! NO NEED TO FEAR!
IT'S CELEBRATED ON THE 31ST OF
OCTOBER, FOR 3 DAYS EACH YEAR.
MAKE SKELETON PUPPETS. THERE'S
NOTHING TO DREAD. WRITE THE NAME
OF A LOVED ONE ON A SUGAR SKULL
HEAD. SAY A PRAYER, LIGHT CANDLES,
FILL BASKETS WITH NUTS, WEAR A
MASK, START TO DANCE, AND
DRINK COCOA IN CUPS.
LEAVE FRUITS,
MARIGOLDS, AND
CANDY ON TOMBSTONES
SO ALL SOULS REVIVE.
THE DAY OF THE DEAD
KEEPS SPIRITS ALIVE!

CALAÇAS
eleton puppet

Make Your Own
Day of the Dead
Mask!

You will need a paper
plate, a felt-tip marker,
string, and scissors.

Draw a skeleton face on
the back of the plate.

Cut out the eyes
and cheeks (with adult
supervision). Punch holes
on the side for the
strings, knot the ends.
Celebrate!

Bones make us tallish, smallish,
a bean pole, a tadpole,
oversized, undersized,
long-legged, or lumpy,
bone-headed, barrel-chested,
stumpy or bumpy.

Bones come in all sizes, shapes, and amounts,
but in the end,

iT's WHaT's iNsiDe tHat CouNts!

For Don and for Rick
whose beautiful bones we love.

You may learn more about Bonz and Higashi Glaser Design at www.zolo.com

Design: Byron Glaser & Sandra Higashi

Library of Congress Control Number:
2003104540

ISBN 0810945991

Published in 2003 by Harry N. Abrams, Incorporated, New York.
All rights reserved. No part of the contents of this book may be reproduced
without the written permission of the publisher.
Printed and bound in Hong Kong
10 9 8 7 6 5 4 3 2 1

HARRY N. ABRAMS, INC.
100 FIFTH AVENUE
NEW YORK, N.Y. 10011
www.abramsbooks.com

Abrams is a subsidiary of

LA MARTINIÈRE
GROUPE